RAINY MORNING

written by **Daniel Pinkwater**

illustrated by **Jill Pinkwater**

ATHENEUM BOOKS FOR YOUNG READERS

Some helpful translations:

Vielen Dank, Frau Submarine. Thank you, Mrs. Submarine.

Bitte, und auch einen corn muffin. Please, and also a *maisgebäck*.

Ja, es regnet. Yes, it's pouring.

Ja, ich glaube. Yes, I do believe so.

Atheneum Books for Young Readers
An imprint of Simon & Schuster's Children's Publishing Division
1230 Avenue of the Americas
New York, New York 10020

Text copyright © 1998 by Daniel Pinkwater
Illustrations copyright © 1998 by Jill Pinkwater

Book design by Nina Barnett
Thanks to Irene Uffrecht-Peters for her help with the German.
The text of this book was set in Cantoria
The illustrations are rendered in magical markers
Printed in Hong Kong
First Edition
10 9 8 7 6 5 4 3 2 1

Library of Congress Cataloging in Publication Data:
Pinkwater, Daniel Manus, 1941–
Rainy Morning / written by Daniel Pinkwater; illustrated by
Jill Pinkwater.—1st ed.   p. cm.
Summary: On a rainy morning, Mr. and Mrs. Submarine invite a cat,
dog, coyote, wildebeest, Ludwig van Beethoven, the United States Marine Band,
and others into their home to share their breakfast of tea and corn muffins.
ISBN 0-689-81143-8
[1. Breakfasts—Fiction. 2. Animals—Fiction.] I. Pinkwater, Jill, ill. II. Title.
PZ7.P6335Rai   1998   [E]—dc21   97-22689

FIRST
EDITION

To each other

—D. P. and J. P.

Mr. and Mrs. Submarine were sitting at the kitchen table on a rainy morning.

"Would you like another breakfast, dear?" Mrs. Submarine asked.

"I have had two breakfasts already," Mr. Submarine said. "But it is raining very hard. I will have one more breakfast, please, but just a small one."

"Oh, look!" Mrs. Submarine said. "The cat is sitting at the window. The poor thing is all wet. I will let him in."

Mrs. Submarine opened the door and the cat walked in,
dripping. The cat sat near the stove, and Mrs. Submarine gave
him a corn muffin.

"I hear the dog scratching at the door," Mr. Submarine said. "I will let him come in and get warm."

Mr. Submarine opened the door, and the dog walked in, dripping. Mrs. Submarine gave the dog a corn muffin, and he took it to his corner to eat it.

"It is certainly wet outside," Mrs. Submarine said.

"It certainly is," Mr. Submarine said. "Look at the poor horse. He's soaked through."

"Poor horse," said Mrs. Submarine.

"He doesn't look very happy," Mr. Submarine said.

"Shall we let him come in?" Mrs. Submarine asked.

"Just this once," Mr. Submarine said.

"I will make more muffins," Mrs. Submarine said.

Mr. Submarine opened the door and whistled to the horse. The horse walked in, dripping.

"I'm just baking more muffins," Mrs. Submarine told the horse.

"There are crows in the tree," Mr. Submarine said.

"Are they wet?" Mrs. Submarine asked.

"They don't look happy," Mr. Submarine said.

"Crows love corn muffins," Mrs. Submarine said.

"I'm going to let them in," Mr. Submarine said.

Mr. Submarine opened the door, and the crows walked in, dripping. They sat on the backs of chairs and ate the corn muffins Mrs. Submarine gave them.

"It certainly is coming down out there," Mr. Submarine said.

"It's an awful morning," Mrs. Submarine said. "Would you like honey in your tea?"

"I would," Mr. Submarine said. "Do you know what I see outside in the rain?"

"What?" Mrs. Submarine asked.

"A wild coyote," Mr. Submarine said.

"As I live and breathe," Mrs. Submarine said. "Is it wet?"

"Oh, very wet," Mr. Submarine said. "Do you suppose it would like to come in?"

"You'd better tempt it with a piece of corn muffin," Mrs. Submarine said. "It might be shy."

Mr. Submarine opened the door and showed the wild
coyote a piece of corn muffin. The coyote walked in, dripping,
and went to lie down under the sink.

"When I was letting the coyote in, do you know what I
saw?" Mr. Submarine asked.

"Something wet?" Mrs. Submarine asked.

"It is the chickens from across the street. They are huddled under a bush."

"Poor things," Mrs. Submarine said. "Better let them in. I will make more muffins."

The chickens walked in, dripping. They huddled in the corner, as far as they could get from the coyote.

"I'm going to bring the car in," Mr. Submarine said.

"All right, dear," Mrs. Submarine said. "Be careful not to run over the chickens."

Mr. Submarine drove the car in, dripping. "I can give it a good wiping with towels while we wait for it to stop raining."

Mr. Submarine busily dried off the car, while the cat, the dog, the horse, the crows, the coyote, and the chickens nibbled corn muffins and got warm and dry.

"There's something outside," Mrs. Submarine said. "I think it's a wildebeest."

"I'll go get it," Mr. Submarine said.

The wildebeest walked in, dripping.

"I'm mixing up more muffins," Mrs. Submarine said.

Mr. Submarine looked out the window. "Now that's unusual!" he said. "It looks like Ludwig van Beethoven is in our yard, soaking wet."

"Oh, invite him in!" Mrs. Submarine said. "He is my favorite composer."

Mr. Submarine pulled on his raincoat and went outside. He came back leading Ludwig van Beethoven by the hand. Beethoven was dripping.

"*Vielen Dank, Frau Submarine,*" Ludwig van Beethoven said.

"Would you like a cup of tea, Herr Beethoven?" Mrs. Submarine asked.

"*Bitte, und auch einen* corn muffin," Beethoven said.

Beethoven got a couple of crows to move to the back of another chair and sat down at the kitchen table.

"Terrible weather this morning," Mr. Submarine said.

"*Ja, es regnet*," Beethoven said.

Ludwig van Beethoven and Mr. Submarine looked out the window at the rain.

"Herr Beethoven, is that the United States Marine Band standing in our yard?" Mr. Submarine asked.

"*Ja, ich glaube,*" Beethoven said.

"I'm glad we bought four hundred and fifty pounds of muffin mix," Mrs. Submarine said. "Ask them to come in."

The United States Marine Band walked in, dripping. The bandsmen shook hands with Ludwig van Beethoven and petted the horse.

"Corn muffins coming up in just a minute!" Mrs. Submarine said.

"Dear, there is a circus in the yard," Mr. Submarine said.

"Oh, no! We do not have room enough for a whole circus!" Mrs. Submarine said.

"It is a small European circus," Mr. Submarine said. "Mostly tumblers and jugglers and clowns. The largest animal they have appears to be a small bear."

"No elephants?" Mrs. Submarine asked.

"None that I can see," Mr. Submarine said.

"Well, that is different, of course," Mrs. Submarine said. "They may come in."

The small European circus walked in, dripping.

Mr. and Mrs. Submarine, and all the animals, and Ludwig van Beethoven, and the United States Marine Band, and the small European circus, ate corn muffins and drank tea in the warm cozy kitchen until the sun came out.